A NOE NOVELLA

The Therapist Chair

PTRD – The End Is A New Beginning

Nicol McClendon

The Therapist Chair: PTRD – The End Is A New Beginning
A NOE Novella
Copyright © 2025 Nicol McClendon
Published by NM Publishing LLC – Candy's Legacy

First Printing 2025

ISBN: 978-1-7359046-1-0 (pbk)
ISBN: 978-1-7359046-2-7 (ebook)

Library of Congress Control Number: 15039536591

*"Dedicated to TJM and the seasons of romance
that cradled me between the illusion of safety and
the ache of unpredictability—the love I gave my
heart to, believing it was forever, but wasn't."*

What if your healing had a voice, and it talked back?

Contents

Act I

The Origin

*Where survival begins
and silence speaks.*

Nicol

I was a young widow. My husband, the love of my life, was taken by gun violence. Nineteen years of my life wiped out in an instant by a coward with a gun.

I couldn't grieve, not really. There was no time for that. I was newly single. I was suddenly all alone in every decision. A mother of three, responsible for the house, the bills, and everything that had once been shared. Survival became my default mode. I had to be fierce, protective. My children had to feel safe, no matter what. Anyone who looked like they threatened that safety better step lightly — or better yet, step away completely.

When you don't allow yourself to grieve after a major life change, especially one as sudden and violent as losing a spouse, the feelings don't disappear. They get shoved into the back of the mind's closet, tucked away beneath layers of responsibilities and deadlines. Who has time to heal? Who has time to be soft? Who has the luxury of unpacking years of heartache when the person you were supposed to spend your life with is gone, taken before their time?

And there's the unspoken pressure. Everyone is watching. Judging. Waiting for you to crack. Waiting for you to show weakness. At least, that's how it feels.

So my grieving process was short, private, and quiet. I knew I needed therapy not just to process the trauma of my husband's death, but to untangle the trauma of surviving it. I went briefly, just enough to satisfy a disability claim at work. Then I ventured out to live a part of the life I had only dreamed of, or at least the life I had seen others living. They call it FOMO: fear of missing out.

The truth? There were parts of life I had missed because I had been a young, somewhat sheltered mother and wife. And when my husband died, there were people who didn't even know I existed. At his funeral, some fool had the audacity to ask where I had been all those years, and how my existence could have gone unnoticed.

I simply replied, "He didn't want the world to know us."

So yes, maybe I had missed out or maybe the world had missed out on me.

I wasn't quite confident being out alone yet, but I faked it until I made it. I ventured out, exploring the world I thought had passed me by, learning who I was outside the shadow of my loss. No one prepares you for grief. There are no classes, no lessons, no manuals for how to continue living when someone you love is gone.

And loss comes in many forms, not only death. Breakups, divorces, and sudden endings are all losses too: the loss of a relationship, the loss of the future you imagined, the loss of comfort, familiarity, or safety.

Often, it's not the present moment that stings the most; it's the dream of what could have been, the future you thought was yours.

No one prepares you for that. Even knowing that life is finite, that relationships can't always last, we rarely take proactive steps to prepare ourselves for the inevitable heartbreak. Therapy is reactive; it forces you to confront what you weren't ready for.

Without therapy, coping mechanisms take over. They don't heal, they bury. Distraction, denial, and pretending (I call it masking) provide temporary relief but never true recovery.

What I didn't know then, but understand now, is that heartbreak has symptoms, real ones, and they don't always show up as tears.

Eventually, the hurt must be faced. You must understand its impact, mend your heart, and start to heal from the side effects of loss and heartbreak.

Sometimes the symptoms look like silence, overthinking, hyper-independence, or the inability to trust love again.

There's a name for it: **Post-Traumatic Relationship Disorder (PTRD)**

Healing doesn't mean forgetting. Sometimes, symptoms of PTRD look like flashbacks to traumatic events in a relationship.

The end wasn't just an ending, it was the beginning of me.

Act II

The Illusion

*When freedom
feels close but
costs everything.*

(1)

She showed up in my life at a time when, I guess, the universe decided I needed adventure, or maybe just a mirror.

She brought out a side of me I didn't even know existed. Or maybe I did know, and she just gave me permission to finally let her breathe.

There was something about her that whispered rebellion. She was the kind of woman who didn't ask for permission, didn't explain herself, didn't apologize for the way her laughter filled a room. She had the kind of confidence that made people look twice, half in admiration, half in fear.

She didn't just walk into a space; she claimed it.

People like to say they don't need validation, but I've learned that most people who say that are actually begging for it, just in reverse. They want validation for being the kind of person who doesn't need validation. It's twisted, but it's true. I've seen it. Hell, I've lived it.

But she wasn't like that. She just… existed. No explanations, no filters, no performances. She was pure energy, free from expectations, free from consequences. That was the terrifying part, because for every wild, beautiful moment she created, I was the one left to clean it up. She left the accountability part of life on the table and sashayed right into the next adventure while I stood in the aftermath, sweeping up the glitter and the broken glass.

But still, I needed her. And in some strange way, I think she needed me too.

The night we met or re-met, depending on how you look at it, was a Thursday. My regular night at The Cloud.

I'd been coming there solo for about three months, trying to get comfortable with the sound of my own thoughts. I sat at the bar, same seat, same order: grilled salmon, sweet potato fries, and a side of sweet chili sauce. L, the bartender, already knew my rhythm. He'd have my drink waiting before I even took off my jacket.

That night the place smelled like fried wings and good decisions gone bad. The lighting was low, soft amber, warm enough to blur the edges of loneliness. My playlist in my head was running on autopilot. It was just me, my plate, and my glass.

Then the door opened.

She walked in like a gust of confidence, tight dress, deep-plum color, hugging every curve like it had been sewn on her body. I noticed immediately because it was my kind of dress. She was thick, curvy, soft in all the same places. My first thought was, *Damn, that would look good on me.*

Yup, I'm that girl. I'll compliment another woman while mentally adding her outfit to my online search list. If she tells me where she got it, great. If not, fine. I'll FBI, CIA, Google-image-search that thing until I find it.

Her scent reached me before she even sat down. It was familiar and unforgettable, notes of black currant and pear danced at the top, softened by hints of patchouli and vanilla. It smelled like boldness wrapped in secrets. I couldn't quite name it, but it stirred something deep in my memory, like a whisper from a moment I hadn't yet remembered.

She slid onto the empty stool next to me, scooted in just enough to cross that invisible line between personal space and curiosity. Normally, I would've shifted away, but for some reason, this time, I didn't.

She raised her hand to flag the bartender, two fingers flicked just like mine. I almost laughed out loud. Coincidence, I told myself. Still, it was unsettling watching her move in a rhythm that felt so… familiar.

The bartender came over, nodded, and in a few minutes placed a fresh drink in front of me. I didn't order another one, but I figured maybe he was just topping me off.

Then I heard it.

"You're welcome," she said, her voice smooth but playful.

I turned to look at her, head tilted, lips pursed in that way I do when I'm silently saying *Don't start with me.*

She laughed. "Yeah, okay."

I put my fork down. *This bih trippin'.*

When I was done eating, I wiped my mouth and took a slow sip of the drink she'd apparently bought.

"This is good," I said, loud enough for her to hear. "And by the way, am I thanking you for this? Is that what you meant by 'you're welcome'?"

She nodded. "Yep. You looked like you needed a refill. I didn't want to drink alone."

"Is that right?"

"Hi," she said, standing now, extending her hand. "I'm Swez. The drink's a token of our new friendship."

Something about her confidence made it hard to say no. I stood, smiled, shook her hand. "Ni.'"

We clinked glasses, and for a moment, the air between us felt charged, like static before a storm.

Then her song came on. K. Cole's *Where He Wanna Be*. She threw her hands up, chair spinning halfway toward the dance floor. I couldn't help but laugh because it was my song too. Next thing I know, she grabs my hand, and we're out there two-stepping like we'd known each other for years.

We danced until our edges blurred, until sweat glistened on our foreheads and the DJ's set became the heartbeat of the night. I hadn't moved like that in forever: uninhibited, alive, unself-conscious.

When I finally sat down, catching my breath, I looked at my watch. Three hours had vanished. I was supposed to be home an hour ago.

As I grabbed my purse, I told her, "I'm usually here on Thursdays."

She smiled, slow and knowing. "I know. You're here every Thursday. I'll see you next week."

We didn't exchange numbers, no socials, no nothing. Just that.

Thursday arrived quicker than I expected. Work dragged, but something in me felt lighter than it had in weeks. When I walked past my closet, I noticed a dress laid out on my bed, a blue one I hadn't even worn yet. I didn't remember pulling it out, but somehow it matched the mood. It fit the night.

When I got to The Cloud, I didn't have to look for her. I smelled her before I saw her, black currant, pear, patchouli. She slid into the stool beside me, flicked those same two fingers, ordered a drink for both of us, and smiled.

That became our rhythm.
Every Thursday.
Same bar, same seat, same ritual.

We never exchanged numbers, never texted, never hung out outside that space. But she always left me something, notes tucked under my windshield wiper.

Her handwriting was clean and sharp, with little hearts over the *i's*:

"Ni', I had a wonderful time. We will do it again. Love, Swez."

Each week, her notes carried something I needed to hear: *Keep going. You're glowing. Stop doubting yourself.*

She knew the right words before I knew I needed them.

And slowly, I started to change.

New hair colors. New lip shades. Dresses instead of jeans. I started to feel alive again, bold, magnetic, lighter. I'd dance more, laugh louder. I started to look forward to Thursdays like a heartbeat.

Somewhere between the drinks, the laughter, and the music, I started to forget that she'd just… appeared. I stopped questioning it.

Until she vanished.

Just as suddenly as she came, she was gone.

The next Thursday, I sat alone at the bar, waiting. L brought my drink, same as always, but it felt different. I kept glancing at the door, expecting that familiar scent to drift in, expecting to see her reflection beside mine in the mirror behind the bar.

But she never showed up.

When I left that night, there was no note on my car, just my reflection in the windshield, eyes lined, lips painted, hair curled… looking more like her than me.

It wasn't until almost a year later, sitting in therapy, that I realized who Swez had really been.

(2)

The room smelled faintly of lavender and wood polish. My therapist's office always felt like a safe little pocket of calm in a world that refused to slow down. There were soft beige walls, a large abstract painting that looked like peace had spilled itself onto a canvas, and that same leather chair that squeaked a little every time I sat down, a sound that, by now, had become strangely comforting.

She smiled when I walked in, that knowing kind of smile she gave when she could tell I had a story to unload.

"Rough week?" she asked, crossing her legs and setting her notepad down, pen resting between her fingers.

"Not rough," I said, sighing as I eased back into the chair. "Just… interesting."

Her eyebrow lifted with the *go on* look.

"So, I met someone," I began. "Well, not really met her… more like she appeared in my life."

She leaned forward slightly, her tone gentle. "Appeared?"

"Yeah." I let out a short laugh. "That sounds crazy, huh? But it's true. Her name's Swez."

"And who is Swez?"

That was the question that always got me. *Who is she?* I thought about the smoky bar lights, the bassline pulsing through our laughter, the way she smelled like something I already knew but couldn't name. The notes she left me, the energy she carried, the fearlessness.

"She's… everything I'm not," I finally said. "Or at least, everything I wasn't. Confident. Wild. Untouchable. She just… doesn't care what people think. She walks in a room, and it's like she owns it, not arrogantly, just with certainty. Like she's free."

My therapist nodded, jotting something down. "And how do you feel when you're around her?"

I thought about that for a second. "Alive. Seen. Unapologetic. Like I don't have to edit myself for anyone."

She tilted her head slightly. "That sounds like a beautiful friendship."

"It was," I said. "Except… I never saw her outside the bar. Never had her number. She just… showed up. Every Thursday. Like clockwork."

A small crease appeared between my therapist's brows, but she didn't interrupt.

"She'd buy me drinks, leave me notes on my windshield, encourage me. Every week, her words just… fit. Like she knew what I was going through." I paused, the thought hitting me in waves. "Actually, she did know. She always knew."

The therapist leaned back, silent, letting me sit in the space between my words. I hated it when she did that. That quiet where your thoughts echo loud enough to hear the truth you don't want to say.

"You said she just… appeared," she said softly. "Do you remember the first time?"

"Yeah. I was sitting at the bar, eating salmon and sweet-potato fries, same as always. She walked in wearing this cute little dress, smelling like patchouli and vanilla. Sat down right next to me and ordered a drink for both of us. Said, 'You're welcome,' like she'd known me all her life."

"And you said you'd never seen her before?"

"Never," I said quickly. But then I hesitated. "I mean… she looked familiar. Her gestures. The way she flicked her fingers for the bartender. Even the way she laughed. It all felt familiar."

She nodded again. "What did she look like?"

I closed my eyes, picturing her. The full figure, the curves, the laugh lines, the spark behind her eyes. I could see her so clearly it almost hurt. "She looked like me," I whispered.

The therapist didn't react, didn't flinch, just let that silence stretch.

Then she asked quietly, "And what does it feel like to say that out loud?"

I blinked, trying to laugh it off. "Weird. Like… I sound delusional. But I swear, she was real. She was sitting right next to me. Other people saw her!"

"Did they?" she asked softly. "Or did they see you?"

The words landed like a slow-burning fuse. I stared at the wall, then at the painting, then back at her.

She spoke again. "You said you felt alive with her, free, seen. You also said she doesn't carry accountability. That part you handle. What if," she paused, her tone careful but firm, "what if Swez is the part of you that you've kept hidden? The one that needed permission to breathe?"

I swallowed hard. "You're saying I made her up?"

"I'm saying maybe you created space for her… space for you, to exist without fear."

My chest tightened, not from sadness but from realization. All those nights, all those notes, all that laughter that felt like healing, maybe it wasn't her rescuing me.

Maybe it was me saving myself.

Tears pricked at the corners of my eyes before I could stop them. I leaned forward, elbows on knees, head bowed. "So, I'm Swez?"

"You are Swez," she said gently. "And Nicol."

For the first time in a long time, I didn't resist the tears. I let them fall. Because maybe I needed to meet myself in that bar. Maybe I needed to dance myself free.

She passed me the tissue box and smiled, that same knowing smile from the beginning of the session.

"You know," she said softly, "you've been meeting yourself every Thursday. You just didn't realize it yet."

I laughed through the tears. "Damn, that's deep."

She laughed too. "Growth usually is."

As I left her office, I couldn't help but think aloud, "If that part of me could show up unannounced, what else was waiting to be seen?"

Act III

The Mirror

The reflection that changes everything.

(3)

She never wrote anything down during our first few sessions.

At least, not where I could see it.

That used to bother me. I wanted proof she was listening, some physical record of my words. But instead, she just sat there: legs crossed, hands resting loosely in her lap, her expression calm but alert.

When she finally did pick up her pen, she didn't take notes about what I said. She wrote down what I avoided.

That's what made her different.

Other therapists I'd tried wanted timelines, symptoms, and coping tools. She wanted truth, the kind that sits just below the surface, pretending to be healed.

She had this way of listening that made silence feel productive. I'd fill the space with nervous chatter until she tilted her head, and suddenly I'd hear myself rambling in circles. That tilt, it was her way of handing me a mirror.

She once said, "You don't have to rush your healing. It's not an appointment you can miss."

I wrote that down as soon as I got to my car.

She called me on my patterns without judgment, the overexplaining, the apologizing, and the need to make sense of chaos by turning it into lessons too soon. She said it was my brain trying to protect me from sitting in discomfort.

"Your feelings don't need to be neat to be valid," she told me. "Sometimes healing looks like falling apart on purpose."

She never coddled me, but she never shamed me either. She showed me grace. She talked to me nice.

She gave me homework sometimes, nothing clinical, just human things:

Listen to a song that used to hurt and notice what it feels like now.

Write a letter you don't plan to send.
Answer yourself out loud when you think something kind.

Simple, but powerful.

Over time, I realized she wasn't trying to fix me. She was teaching me to sit with myself long enough to remember I didn't need fixing.

That's what made the Swez session hit harder.
She didn't tell me who Swez was. She led me there.

Even after the tears, the laughter, the long pauses filled with realization, she stayed still, steady, like a lighthouse that doesn't chase the boats; it just shines.

And somehow, in that stillness, I found my way back to shore.

(4)

I sat in my car for a long while after that session, engine off, keys dangling between my fingers. The late afternoon sun was hanging low, pouring gold through the windshield like the universe wanted to spotlight my realization: *I am Swez.*

It sounded strange at first, almost foreign. My breath caught, not in panic but in awe, then it began to settle inside me like a truth that had been waiting for its turn to speak. I ran my fingers over the steering wheel. Feeling every worn groove. Every small imperfection. The same way I was learning to feel myself. All my edges, my softness, my contradictions.

I thought about those Thursday nights at the bar. The laughter, the songs, the outfits I couldn't remember buying. How I had always left lighter than I came. How I felt seen by someone who didn't demand an explanation for my joy.

It was me all along.

The parts of me that therapy had been trying to coax out, confidence, freedom, presence, had simply found another way to live.

Swez wasn't an illusion. She was a manifestation.

A permission slip I wrote myself.

For so long, I had lived small. Careful. Always expecting the next disappointment, always afraid to take up too much space, to be too much of anything. Swez showed up to remind me that *too much* is just what people call you when they cannot contain your light.

She showed me how to live on my own terms, to dance, to be seen, to laugh with my whole chest again. And when I was ready to live that way without her permission, she disappeared. Maybe she never left. Maybe she just stepped back inside me where she always belonged.

The therapist was right. I'd been meeting myself every Thursday night. And now maybe I didn't need the bar to find her anymore.

I turned on the ignition and rolled down the window. The breeze came through, soft and cool, brushing against my skin like a quiet affirmation.

For the first time, I didn't feel divided. I felt whole.

I whispered to the empty car, to the reflection staring back at me in the rearview mirror, "Hey, Swez."

And for the first time, she smiled back.

Peace feels good, almost too good. And that's usually when life decides to test it.

(5)

Mornings felt different after that.

Not dramatic or cinematic. Just lighter. I wasn't waking up searching for something to fix or someone to love me back into balance. My peace wasn't loud anymore. It was steady, warm, calm breathing and loosened shoulders. The kind that hums quietly in the background while you're making coffee or folding laundry.

I'd catch glimpses of myself in the mirror sometimes, not checking for flaws or angles, just *seeing.*

There she was. Both of us. The woman who had been through the fire and the one who danced through the smoke. The soft and the steel.

Therapy taught me that healing isn't about becoming someone new. It's about remembering who you were before the world told you who to be.

And for the first time in a long time, I didn't need to prove anything to anyone. Not even to myself.

I started spending my Thursdays differently. Still dressed up, still with a little perfume and gloss, but not waiting for someone to appear or fill a space. Sometimes I went to The Cloud. Sometimes I stayed home. Sometimes I poured a glass of wine, turned on music, and danced in my kitchen. Alone, but not lonely.

I noticed the silence stopped feeling like punishment and started feeling like peace. My reflection no longer startled me; the woman looking back didn't flinch when she held her own gaze.

The next time I saw my therapist, she smiled before I even sat down. "You look different," she said.

"I feel different," I replied.

It wasn't a transformation. It was a return.

The Unraveling

*Threads loosen,
and truths demand
to be heard.*

(6)

It always happens when you least expect it.

The universe has a funny way of checking your progress, not through tests you can prepare for, but through people you thought you'd already graduated from.

I ran into him at the grocery store. Of all places, Stop and Shop. Hair up, sweats on, lip gloss barely hanging on after a long day.

I was midway through the produce aisle, my cart nearly empty, just a few essentials: bananas, strawberries, and pineapples. I stood there, debating between spinach or kale, when I heard that familiar voice. Unmistakable. Right behind me.

"Ni'? Is that you?"

My body froze before my mind could catch up. That tone. Soft. Familiar. Like he was picking up a conversation that never ended. I turned around slowly. There he was.

The one who used to make my heart race, and my voice soften.

The one who had once promised me *a couple of forevers*. The one who had left me questioning everything.

Yup, it was *Him*, standing in front of me, looking like a lesson I'd already learned.

He looked the same, maybe a little more tired around the eyes. Time hadn't been unkind to him, just honest. He smiled the way he used to. But it didn't hit the same this time.

"You look good." he said, stepping closer.

"Hey. Thanks" I said simply, tucking a loose curl behind my ear. "You too."

My voice was even, not that trembling mix of anger and nostalgia that used to live in my throat whenever his name came up. The words felt polite, not charged. Calm.

My pulse didn't spike. My stomach didn't twist. It was like running into a song you used to love until you finally understood the lyrics weren't about you.

He glanced at my cart. "Still picky about fruit, huh?"
"Still observant, I see."

He laughed softly, that laugh that once melted all my boundaries.
It didn't anymore.

"So… how have you been?" he asked, voice dipped in small talk and maybe a little regret.

I shrugged, smiling a little. "I've been good. Better, actually. Peaceful."

He nodded, maybe a little surprised. "You always did land on your feet."

"Sometimes I had to crawl first."

He nodded like he didn't quite believe it. "You still dancing?"

"Always." I smiled, a real one this time. "Just not to the same tune."

He smiled again, slower this time, studying me like I'd changed languages.

"You seem … different."

"I am," I said simply.
And it's not up for negotiation this time.

He looked me up and down, like he was searching for the version of me he used to know. The one who loved too loudly and forgave too easily. She wasn't there.

There was a time I would've filled that silence with explanations, who I'd become, how I'd healed, what I'd learned. But I didn't owe him the translation.

He shifted his weight, trying to read me the way he used to, but those pages were closed now.

"You still go to The Cloud?" he asked.

"Sometimes," I said. "But not for the same reasons."

He looked like he wanted to ask what that meant but decided against it. Instead, he gave a small nod, the kind that says *I get it,* even when they don't.

There was an awkward pause. The kind where the air gets heavy with everything unspoken. We smiled, polite and distant, like two people who had shared a chapter but now lived in different books.

I could feel the ghost of old conversations hovering between us, the apologies that never came, the closure I thought I needed.
But I didn't feel the pull this time.

He laughed softly, but there was something in his eyes, confusion, curiosity, maybe both.

He was used to me trying, reaching, filling the silence with emotions. But I didn't owe him any of that anymore.

For the first time, I wasn't trying to be understood.
I was just standing there, whole, grounded, unbothered.

Swez was there too but not separate from me this time. She was the steady rhythm in my chest, the quiet confidence behind my calm.

He shifted on his feet, realizing the moment wasn't going to turn into what it used to.

"Well," he said, "it was good seeing you, Ni."

"You too," I replied.
And I meant it, but not in the way I used to.

As I walked away, I didn't look back.
Not because I was trying to be strong, but because I
didn't need to anymore.

That's when I realized I was still holding the spinach. I
dropped it in the cart, pushed forward, and whispered
under my breath,
"Look at you, Ni'. Choosing what's good for you."

There was no urge to replay the encounter.
No ache in my stomach.
No imaginary conversations running in my head.

Just silence.
Peaceful, grown-woman silence.

When I got home, I kicked off my shoes, poured myself
a glass of wine, and turned on some music, not the sad
songs this time, something smooth, confident, free.

I caught my reflection in the window, hair a little messy,
smile soft but sure.

And I felt her again.

Swez. Me. Us.
No longer two women fighting for space.
Just one woman finally living in her truth.

Later that night, I sat in bed with my journal open, pen tapping against the page. The words came easy this time, not heavy, not rushed. Just honest.

I saw him today.
And I didn't crumble.

I finally realized healing wasn't about pretending something never happened. It's about no longer needing it to end differently.

Seeing him reminded me of how much I had grown, not from what he did or didn't do, but from what I'd finally given myself: love, grace, permission.

I used to chase peace like it was hiding from me.
But now, peace is the one waiting patiently while I remember I am already home.

Swez taught me how to live without apology.
Therapy taught me how to stay accountable for that freedom.
And somewhere between the two, I found myself, the woman who no longer flinches when she is seen.

I closed the journal and turned off the light, whispering one last thought into the dark:

"I did not lose him. I found me."

The idea of love changed.
I started to believe that love was not loud, not chaotic,
not the kind that burns fast and leaves ashes behind.
It should feel gentle, like a slow sunrise, quiet but
undeniable.

I was not searching for forever anymore.
I was learning to just be present in moments that felt
like peace.

It had been months since that day in the grocery store.
The memory doesn't sting; it hums.
A small reminder of a woman I used to be, the one
who believed love was earned through effort, through
proving, through performance.

Love was supposed to meet me where I stood.
Not chase me.
Not save me.
Just see me.

(7)

I've been watching her from a distance. Waiting for the perfect moment to reappear.

That moment when Nicol was too deep in her soft era to remember her power, that's when I always show up.

The moment she needed me the most.

I've watched her go to all those sessions after I left, journaling, crying, unlearning, but still forgetting the basics.

She's that girl.

I believe her need for softness is starting to make her feel small again.

Making her forget her edge.
Therapy taught her peace;

I reminded her she's power.

Welp, let me get my tea and use the bathroom before *Life* got here, because Nicol got me on the edge like always. *Life* always showed up on time… And we all know *"Life Be Lifing."*

Act V

The Pause

The stillness that reshapes the soul.

Years after meeting Swez, I finally allowed myself a pause.

Not to escape life, but to feel it.

After all the masks, the performances, and the rebuilding, I needed a moment to breathe.

When my husband died, I became everything to everyone, mother, provider, protector.

My children were young at the time; they relied on me completely, and I had no choice but to *"have it."*

I carried the house, the bills, their needs, and my own silent heartbreak, stuffing it into a corner of my chest no one could see.

To the outside world, I was unbreakable. Strong. Fierce.

I had to be.

I smiled through exhaustion, never once letting anyone see me break.

So, for over a decade, if anyone asked, "How are you doing?" my answer was always the same: "I'm okay," or "I got it."

But being strong was not a flex, it was survival.

And yet, beneath that learned behavior, I was bleeding internally, day after day.

I thought no one noticed, but they did.
My children watched me in those years.

They saw the weight I carried even when I smiled.

They felt it in the quiet moments, the way I flinched at phone calls, or the nights I stayed awake until their breathing evened out, making sure they were safe before I even allowed myself to rest.

They saw the breakdowns I couldn't hide.

They saw their mother, vulnerable yet still present.

That was why I finally decided to start therapy in earnest, not for me alone, but for them.

I wanted them to see a woman who could heal, thrive, and live fully.

The pause was not easy.
It was uncomfortable. Raw. Unforgiving.

But after years of pretending strength was peace. I had to confront the habits and patterns that had protected me but also imprisoned me.

I had to untangle the web of deceit I had created for myself.

I had to face the hyper-independence I had wielded like a sword.

The armor I had carried for decades began to rust and what poured out beneath it was grief.

I had to face myself, unfiltered.

I crumbled.

I stopped running.

And when I did, I realized something critical:

Being strong all the time wasn't survival, it was avoidance.

It was hiding in plain sight.

I sat in the wreckage.

The silence was deafening, but necessary.

I didn't know it then, but this pause would become the bridge to my healing.

Act VI

The Becoming

*Learning to breathe
without fear.*

(8)

One Saturday afternoon, I found myself at a local bookstore café, it was my "new Thursday."

A safe ritual, only this time with books and chai lattes instead of music and martinis.

I was sitting by the window, journal open, when a man asked if the seat next to me was taken.

He did not come with a line or a look, just an easy smile and a coffee that smelled like cinnamon.

I nodded and went back to my writing, but I felt him glance over. Not in the way that demanded attention, but in the way that quietly offered it.

"Are you writing a book?" he asked after a few minutes.

I looked up and smiled. "Maybe. Or maybe it's writing me."

He laughed softly, the kind of laugh that did not fill the room but somehow reached the corners of it.

There was something familiar about his energy.
Calm, self-assured. Not trying to impress. Just present.
He was not engaging in curiosity; he was genuinely interested.

We talked about books, music, and travel. Nothing too deep, but the conversation felt easy, like we had known each other in another life and were just catching up.

At one point, I caught myself checking for old habits: overexplaining, expecting, shrinking.
None of them showed up. It was just me, grounded, curious, whole.

When he asked for my number, I did not feel the old flutter of anxiety or the need to play coy.

I just smiled and said, "Sure."

He handed me his phone, and as I typed in my name, I caught my reflection on the black screen.

For a second, I swore I saw a glimmer of her, *Swez,* smirking back at me. Not separate anymore, just present.

This time, it wasn't a performance.

It was a soft opening —
A chance to let love in without losing myself.

It's strange how peace can feel foreign after you have lived in chaos for so long.

Sometimes I caught myself waiting for the floor to fall through, for the silence to mean distance, for the calm to hide a storm.

That is the thing about being anxious in love. Even when it is good, you scan for danger.

He was steady and consistent. But his quiet, still and contained energy sometimes brushed against the raw edges of my old fear.

I'd catch myself checking his tone, his timing, the space between his texts.

The old me would've spiraled.
The woman I am now… just breathed.

One Thursday night, he canceled dinner at the last minute, said work ran late, promised to make it up to me.

The ache came fast, that old, familiar sting of disappointment blooming in my chest.

I felt the ghost of every *"I'll call you back"* that never came. Every *"It's not you, it's me"* that left me holding the pieces.

But this time, I didn't run with it.
I didn't perform indifference or punish him with silence.

I sat with myself, literally.
Cross-legged on the couch, face bare, phone flipped over.
I took a long breath and whispered, "You're safe."

Because I was.
For the first time, I was safe with me.

That night, I wrote in my journal, not about him, but about the part of me that panicked.

I wanted to understand her.

The little girl inside who learned that love could vanish overnight.
She didn't need to be silenced; she needed to be seen.

A few days later, he showed up with dinner and an apology.

He didn't bring flowers, just eye contact.

And somehow that meant more.

We sat on the floor, eating takeout straight from the containers, and I told him the truth.

Not the pretty version, the raw one.

"I used to make everything about abandonment," I said quietly.
"Any time someone canceled plans or got distant, I'd build a whole story about why I wasn't enough. I'm trying not to do that anymore."

He looked at me for a long moment, then reached across the space between us.

"I get that," he said. "I pull back sometimes when I'm overwhelmed, not because I don't care, but because I was raised to handle things alone. I'm learning too."

That's when it hit me, healing isn't about finding someone perfectly secure.

It's about finding someone willing to meet you in the middle.

Willing to learn your language as you unlearn your fear.

We didn't fix each other that night.

We just told the truth, and that was enough.

Later, when he wrapped his arm around me, my body didn't tense.
I didn't analyze the gesture.
I just leaned in, not because I needed him to hold me together, but because I wanted to share the space.

That's the difference between old love and healed love.

Old love clings to survive.

Healed love breathes.

The following week, I found myself back on that same couch in my therapist's office.
Same soft lighting.
Same plant in the corner that leaned a little too far toward the sun.

She didn't have to ask how I was doing.
She just smiled, knowingly, that therapist smile that says *you've come a long way.*

Still, she waited. She always waited.

"I didn't panic this time," I said finally. "I noticed the feeling, but I didn't let it take the wheel."

She nodded slowly. "That's progress, Nicol. That's the work working."

I laughed. "It felt weirdly calm. Like my body remembered the script, but my spirit refused to act it out."

"Exactly," she said. "You're reprogramming what love feels like. It's not adrenaline anymore. It's safety."

I sat with that word, *safety.*

It sounded so simple, but it had taken me years to find it.
Not in a man, not in a promise, but in myself.

"I think I finally understand," I whispered. "Healing doesn't mean I stop feeling fear or longing. It just means I don't abandon myself when they show up."

She smiled again, softer this time. "That's it. You've learned to stay."

Those words landed like truth.

I'd spent a lifetime leaving myself to chase love that couldn't hold me. Now, I was learning the art of staying, staying through silence, through uncertainty, through softness that didn't require sacrifice.

When I left her office, the air outside felt lighter, almost forgiving.

The city hummed around me, alive and indifferent.

But I didn't feel small anymore. I felt *here*.

I thought of *Him*, the cinnamon coffee, the laughter, the warmth, and for once, I didn't rush to name what we were.
It didn't need a label. It was a mirror. A moment.
A gentle reminder that love, in its purest form, should expand you, not erase you.

As I drove home, the sky was that bruised kind of beautiful that comes just before sunset —the hour where light and shadow dance.

And I realized… that's where I live now.
Not in the extremes. Not in the chaos or the calm.
But right there in the in-between, where peace feels earned and love feels possible.

The kind of place where you can finally say,

"I am enough, even when no one's choosing me."

I turned up the music, something soulful, something familiar, and smiled as the city blurred past.

Not chasing. Not waiting. Just becoming.

Then something beautiful happened...

He changed. Became emotionally available.
Communicated and stayed connected.
We started taking trips, going on dates, just cuddling
on the couch.
He cooked for me. Pleased me in every way.

I think I'm in love.
No, I *know* I am.
He is the one.

(9)

Two years later

The leather chair squeaked as I sank into it, my shoulders heavy from carrying the week like bricks in my backpack. I stared at the little sand timer on her desk, every grain slipping seemed to whisper, let it go, just let it go.

"You've been quiet today," she said, pen poised. "Tell me what's on your mind."

I laughed, a little bitter, and leaned back. "Where do I even start? It's like I keep showing up, expecting people to meet me halfway, and they never do."

Her eyes softened. "Because you give so much," she said, "and maybe you're expecting them to give what you can't control. You've been giving your love to the wrong containers, Ni.'"

I nodded slowly, feeling a lump in my throat. The truth stung. I'd always known I loved fiercely, too fiercely, maybe. But hearing it out loud made it real.

"I keep thinking about *Him*," I said, voice low. "And how I wanted forever. How I needed forever. And he… he just, he couldn't."

My fingers fidgeted with the edge of my jeans. "I don't even know if he loved me. Or if he just loved the way I loved him."

She didn't rush to answer. She let the silence stretch. And in that pause, I realized the depth of my own wanting, not just for him, but for someone, anyone, to see me completely. To not flinch at my intensity.

"You're grieving what you never had," she said finally. "And that's valid. But grieving isn't about him. It's about understanding why you gave so much to someone incapable of receiving it."

I exhaled, letting some tension slip. Therapy had a way of untangling the knots without me even noticing, each session, a slow peeling of layers I didn't know I'd been holding onto.

"And Swez," I said, almost laughing at the memory, "she showed up when I needed her. Like magic. No explanations, no expectations. Just… a wild, free version of me that I didn't know I was allowed to be."

She smiled knowingly. "That's the part of you you've been hiding, Ni'. Seeing that side of yourself, fully alive, is going to be uncomfortable. Because you're realizing you've been holding yourself back for everyone else."

I sank further into the chair, imagining Swez's energy, effortless, unapologetic, untethered. I wanted that for myself. Maybe therapy wasn't about changing people; maybe it was about changing the way I loved, and how I allowed myself to be loved.

"Next week," she said, standing and gathering her notes, "we're going to explore your attachment patterns. I want you to start seeing why you chase people who can't chase you back."

I nodded, a shiver of both fear and excitement running down my spine.

"I wasn't afraid of being alone anymore; I was afraid of never being known."

Change was uncomfortable, yes, but the thought of finally being seen on my own terms… that was worth every awkward, painful, raw minute of this work.

Act VII

The Reckoning

Facing the patterns that held me captive.

(10)

She was late for our session. I hated tardiness, and I had no patience. My schedule was full today. It didn't matter what time she arrived; I was billing her for the full hour, and she'd be leaving at 3 p.m. because my next client *Life* was always on time for her appointment, 3:15pm sharp. I had to get my tea and use the bathroom before *Life* got here anyway, because *Life* had me on edge like always. And we all know *"Life Be Lifing."*

Nostalgia walked in like she was early. Actually, she walked in like I was her client. I just looked at her and shook my head. She plopped down on my chaise. I turned on my recorder. She moved slowly, removed her shoes, and let out a long, deliberate sigh.

Something was wrong. I could tell immediately. But I spared her my usual tongue-lashing. Nope. I would save that venom for another day.

I put my glasses on, the same way I always had for the last two years, and she started to speak.

"Imagine waking up so full of resentment. Imagine someone hugging you so tightly you can feel them trying to extract every bit of pain from your body, but you cannot, no, you would not, release it. Imagine someone whispering in your ear, 'You deserve the world,' then screaming, 'NOW FOCUS!' because they can tell you don't want to try again. Imagine thinking, I'm so broken, no one can fix this."

I said, "Imagine letting go, because forgiveness isn't for them, it's for you."

She rolled her eyes.

Nostalgia and I were always at odds, bumping heads on everything. Nevertheless, I genuinely loved her. Our relationship never went beyond the therapist chair, but I cared.

I told her to start at the beginning. The only way to treat her disorder and end the pain was to start there.

Nostalgia began to speak... I wasn't even paying attention at first. Then it hit me. I looked up, and I was in too deep, so deep it felt like floating on a cloud, covered in this overwhelming love.

Nostalgia always had a way with words. Her stories moved like they had weight, like you could see them in the air as she spoke. She required my full attention. I preferred writing notes during sessions, but Nostalgia demanded eye contact. That's why I started using a recorder.

She continued:

"Yeah, I was floating. I had the time of my life. I've never been swept off my feet like that. He showed me so much love and gentle care. For two years, we were inseparable. I just could not imagine anything going wrong when everything was so right."

Then she paused. Longer than her usual for dramatic effect. I could see her eyes filling with water.

"So, what changed?" I asked.

"No," she said, shaking her head. "It's not what changed. It's how things stayed the same."

Her man, *Him,* had come up before in sessions. She was happy. I thought she was healing.

One day, she came in dressed to the nines, smelling divine, skipping in like the world owed her something. She wanted to cut the session short, knowing full well I would still bill her the full hour. She was going out with *Him*. I smiled, happy for her.

Love was rare in my practice. Many women had shut the door to it forever, scarred by betrayal, rejection and lies. But Nostalgia seemed genuine. The love she felt for *Him* was alive again, unlocked.

That session was her breakthrough. Her eyes sparkled. Her words poured out:

"You know there's something about a man who is emotionally available. A man who loves to communicate and stay connected. I can't get enough of *Him*. He never wants to leave me. We've taken trips, we go on dates, even just cuddle on the couch. He cooks for me and pleases me in every way. We complement each other. I think I'm in love. No, I know I am. He is the one."

She shared their plans for marriage, the certainty of their connection, and the gratitude she felt for having found *Him* after giving up hope.

I didn't worry at first. I reminded myself, she was my client, not my friend. But my concern began when she started cutting sessions short, then missing them entirely. Also, therapy wasn't her idea. It was a condition of her release, stamped in bold ink by a judge who probably thought healing could be scheduled like a dentist appointment.

So, I called her.

"Hey Nostalgia, what's going on? You can't keep missing sessions. It's vital for your mental health and yeah, I know, it's court-mandated too, but we'll unpack that part later. Just know I'll have to report it if this keeps up."

She sighed on the other end, that kind of sigh that carries both defiance and exhaustion.

She apologized, promising she would come to the next full session.

The day arrived. I was in early, setting up. The clock ticked painfully slow.

A chill ran down my spine, I smelled her before I saw her.

She entered, radiating pain yet still beautiful.

She carried a small bag in her right hand, weighed down at the center, her nails digging into it. Her left hand sported a diamond eternity band.

She sat on my chaise, shoes off, silent.

I noticed immediately, there was no smile, and her shoulders were slumped.

I switched on the recorder.

She spoke:

"Imagine waking up so full of resentment. Imagine someone hugging you so tightly you can feel them trying to extract every bit of pain from your body, but you couldn't, no, you wouldn't, release it. Imagine someone whispering in your ear, 'You deserve the world,' then screaming, 'NOW FOCUS!' because they can tell you didn't want to try again. Imagine thinking, I'm so broken, no one can fix this."

Something about her words felt familiar. Like I had heard them before... recently.

I said, "Imagine letting go of all the hurt, rejection, and lies. Forgive and move on. Forgiveness isn't for them, it's for you."

She stared through me. As if she could see my own broken heart.

"There is no forgiveness," she said. "You cannot help me."

She set the bag on the table, released her fist, put on her shoes, and stood.

"I'm going away now," she said, "but you'll see me again."

I called out, "You're leaving your bag."

She whispered, "What's in there never belonged to me," and walked out.

An envelope taped to the side of the bag caught my attention: one name - NICOL, in all caps.

Inside a letter that read:

"I have a disorder, and there is only one cure. Generic forms work temporarily. Once they stop, they must be disposed of. You told me to tell my story, and I did. Now you must take out your own trash."

Opening the bag, a stench hit me. I gagged. The contents of the bag were horrific.

I dropped the bag, and its contents fell to the floor. I ran to the bathroom, splashing cold water on my face. Looking up, my reflection stared back at me, glasses off, but the handwriting on the letter was unmistakable:

"I searched *Him* for a heart but couldn't find one. I can see yours is broken. Take his brain and try to make sense of all of this. See you soon, Nostalgia."

I stood there for a long moment, staring at the letter in my hand, my mind spinning. The stench lingered like a shadow, crawling into my nose and throat, a grotesque perfume that somehow made the air heavier.

My pulse was loud in my ears, my hands trembling, not from fear, not exactly, but from recognition.

Something about this, no, everything about this, felt too familiar.

I sank into my chair, still holding the letter, and replayed the words in my mind.

"I searched *Him* for a heart but couldn't find one. I can see yours is broken. Take his brain and try to make sense of all of this."

Him. The capitalized pronoun. The obsession. The longing. The perfection. It wasn't just a story of love gone wrong. It was my story.

I didn't notice the recorder had stopped running. I didn't care. I sank lower into the chair and allowed myself to feel the grief, the rage, the shame, and the longing.

All of it.

All the things I'd compartmentalized and stored neatly away for years, all the reasons I had built the walls that made me Nicol, the therapist, the fixer, the voice of reason.

And then it hit me.

I was Nostalgia.

Not figuratively, not metaphorically, not just the echoes of a clients trauma reflecting on my life. I was her, the very same; the resentment, longing, the obsession, the inability to forgive, all of it.

She had been speaking to me, but it *was me* speaking to myself. Yet somehow, through the therapy ritual, I had managed to hide from myself long enough to forget that I was the client in my own chair.

My breath caught. My hands shook violently as I realized the magnitude of it. Weeks, months, maybe years of counseling *her*, guiding *her*, listening to *her* stories, *were really me talking to me.*

I tried to speak, but my voice sounded foreign in my own ears.

"Nostalgia, it's me."

The room went quiet, as if confirming the truth.

My reflection in the mirror on the opposite wall stared back, unblinking, patient, accusatory. The reflection, myself and her, was one and the same.

I could see the small ticks I'd unconsciously mirrored from her.

The sighs.
The pauses.
The little tilt of the head when she was trying to emphasize a point.

I sank onto the chaise fully, the weight of the bag, the stench, the letter, all the guilt, grief, and longing pressing down like a physical force.

I realized now why she had always required my full attention, why she demanded my presence, why she had haunted every session.

She wasn't a client.

She was the part of me I had refused to see.

The revelation was both terrifying and oddly liberating.

I began to speak to the empty room, to the recorder, to the shadows:

"I am Nostalgia. I am every heartbreak I've buried, every obsession I've locked away, every part of me that I promised would never speak again. And yet, here I am. I am the rage, the longing, and the grief I've never processed."

For the first time in years, I allowed tears to fall freely. Not the controlled, tidy tears I let myself cry after a loss or at the end of a session.
These were messy, primal, cleansing tears, the kind that clawed at the raw edges of my soul.

I spoke aloud, "And now, now I have to fix me. Not them. Not Him. Not some fantasy I've been chasing or counseling. Me and only me."

And so the real therapy began.

I sat there in my office, the recorder running, bag of horrors at my feet, and began to ask myself the questions I had asked Nostalgia hundreds of times. Only this time, I had to answer honestly.

"Imagine waking up so full of resentment… Who has tried to extract your pain? Who is holding you hostage with your own story? Who do you refuse to forgive?"

I was Nostalgia and I was Nicol.
The client and the therapist merged into one.

And for the first time, I realized the truth:
Post-Traumatic Relationship Disorder (PTRD) wasn't just a clinical concept.

It was a map of my own life, a trail of broken love, broken trust, and the fragments of myself I had scattered across time.

And if I wanted to heal, I had to navigate it.
Alone.
But not alone.

Because the part of me that had always been Nostalgia, the part that had carried the story of every hurt, every longing, every betrayal, was ready to speak.

And I was ready to listen.

The ringing of my alarm jolted me back to reality, 3:15pm sharp... *Life* had just shown up. *Life* always showed up on time… And we all know *"Life Be Lifing."*

(11)

Nostalgia didn't walk into therapy on her own. She was court-ordered after an incident that blurred the lines between heartbreak and breakdown.

It started with *Him*, the one she thought was her forever. The one who mirrored her intensity just enough to keep her hooked, but never enough to hold her. Their relationship was a slow unraveling: Passion laced with manipulation, silence weaponized as punishment, and love dangled like bait.

One night, after another disappearing act, she snapped.

She showed up at his place unannounced. Not to fight. Not to beg.

Just to be seen.

But he wasn't alone. The woman who answered the door wore her perfume. Her earrings. Her smile. Nostalgia didn't scream. She didn't cry. She just stood there, frozen, until the woman closed the door in her face.

That night, Nostalgia drove aimlessly for hours. Her phone buzzed with messages from friends, from her kids, from *Him*, who suddenly remembered she existed. She didn't answer. She ended up parked outside his house, staring at the porch light until sunrise.

Neighbors called the police.

The report said disturbance.

The officer said trespassing.

The judge said mandated therapy.

But what Nostalgia heard was: You're broken. You're dangerous. You need fixing.

She didn't believe it at first. She thought therapy was punishment.

A box to check.

A hoop to jump through.

But what she didn't know what she couldn't have known was that therapy wouldn't just be a sentence.

It would be a mirror.

One that would show her not just the pain she carried, but the parts of herself she had buried to survive.

(12)

The office felt different now. The hum of the air conditioner, usually background white noise, felt like a spotlight. I was no longer listening to Nostalgia. I was Nostalgia. Every chair, every shadow, every photograph on the wall became part of me. I ran my fingers over the chaise as if it were a living thing, as if it could remind me who I was and who I had buried.

I turned on the recorder. Not for documentation. Not for accountability. For me. For Nostalgia. For the parts of myself that refused to be silent any longer.

"Why did you leave me?" I whispered into the microphone. My voice cracked, not from weakness, but from recognition.

I could feel the old tension in my chest, the rage I had held for Swez leaving me. For *Him*, every man who had ever promised me forever and left me with fragments. I could feel the grief for my husband, the loss of nineteen years of dreams, stolen, interrupted, obliterated. I could feel the fear I had held for my children, the exhaustion of pretending to be invincible.

I sat upright and asked myself the question I had asked all of my clients:

"What happened that you can't let go?"

And I remembered.

The love I had locked away.

The betrayal I had tried to bury.

The anger I had poured into "fixing others" while refusing to fix myself.

The woman in the mirror.

My clients were my past, my present and the blueprint of my unresolved trauma.

I took a deep breath and let the words tumble out, half confession, half plea:

"I loved *Him*. I still love *Him*. And I hated myself for needing *Him*. I hated myself for loving what didn't want to stay. I hated that I allowed myself to disappear into someone else's life, someone else's story. And I was too blind, too stubborn, too scared to heal. Until now."

I paused. The silence pressed down like a heavy blanket.

And then… I felt it, a presence. Not physically, not in the room, but in the air. A pulse. A shadow of thought. Another voice waiting to speak.

I knew it immediately. This was the next part of me that had been waiting to show up.

I felt her before I saw her. A shift in the room, a tightening in my chest. My hands were clammy. The recorder flickered off then back on, although I hadn't touched it. I closed my eyes and let her take shape.

"Are you ready?" the voice whispered, unmistakably mine, yet not mine.

"I'm ready," I said, and the words tasted foreign on my tongue.

She had come to teach me what I refused to learn. She had been hiding in the shadows of every decision I had made since my husband died. She was the part of me that survived by observation, by manipulation, by control. She had watched Swez and Nostalgia play out their stories, waiting for the moment when I could confront the truth.

The air thickened, and even my breath seemed afraid to move. I reached for the bag, still on the floor from Nostalgia's last visit. The stench had faded, but the memory lingered. I traced the letter with my fingertips and whispered:

"It's time to see the whole truth. All of it."

And just like that, she stepped forward.

Her name was Truth.

(13)

Truth was different, calculated. Cool. Dangerous in a way that demanded attention but commanded control. She moved through memories I hadn't touched, secrets I hadn't acknowledged, truths too sharp to face.

She didn't smile. She doesn't do that.

"Are you sure you're ready?" she asked.

"For what?" I replied, even though I already knew.

"For honesty," she said simply.

The first "session" with Truth was quiet. Too quiet. There was no dramatic entrance, no outburst, no perfume, no shoes removed. Just a sharp, undeniable presence in the corner of my mind.

I asked the question that had begun every therapy session for years:

"Why am I here?"

Truth's answer was a mirror.

"Because you cannot continue to heal the parts of yourself you refuse to acknowledge. You cannot continue to hold Swez and Nostalgia at arm's length while pretending that PTRD is only about others. You are all of them. You have always been all of them."

I swallowed.

"But I don't understand," I whispered. "How... how can this be real?"

"It is as real as every heartbreak, every betrayal, every obsession you've carried," she said. Her voice was calm, hypnotic. "You created us to survive. You split yourself so you could endure. You've been the therapist, the client, the observer. And now... it's time to face the architect."

I sat on the chaise, trembling, realizing that the only person who could save Nostalgia, who could save me, was Nicol herself. Not the "me" who held the office, the credentials, the authority, but the raw, exposed Nicol.

Truth guided me through memories, through the messy and painful edges I had tried to sanitize in every session:

Swez's freedom, my longing to release responsibility. Nostalgia's heartbreak, my own obsession with what I could not control.
Him, the men I had loved and lost, the dreams I had buried, the grief I had refused to name.

And then Truth said:

"You've been hiding from yourself in plain sight. You cannot fix PTRD in others until you fix PTRD in you. Until you reconcile all the alters you've created, all the fragments of pain you've externalized, you will keep carrying the weight of ghosts that aren't even separate from you."

The words sank like a stone in my chest. I realized she was right. Every client I had listened to, every session I had documented, every breakthrough I had witnessed in others, had been preparation. I had been running, avoiding, pretending.

I closed my eyes and let myself feel. For the first time in my life, I didn't compartmentalize. I didn't rationalize. I didn't analyze.

I just let it be.

Act VIII

The Integration

Gathering every fractured piece into wholeness.

(14)

The next week, the office felt heavier. The air was thicker, the candle burning was scented with sandalwood and something bittersweet I couldn't name. I'd been running back-to-back sessions all week, my patience thin as tissue paper, when she walked in, heels clicking, perfume slicing through the fatigue like a blade.

Truth.

Her name alone carried weight. Every session with her was like pulling teeth, messy, painful, necessary. She made my life a living hell, yet I could never let her go. Something about her kept me tethered. Connected.

Truth said, "I really don't know where to begin. There are so many thoughts racing through my mind all the time. I need you to help me organize, categorize, and begin to work through this mess. Isn't that what I'm paying you for, Nicol?"

I sighed, not even hiding my exhaustion. "Something like that," I said, rubbing my temples.

She was my age, well dressed, always smelling divine, notes of amber and jasmine today, if I wasn't mistaken. All of my women smelled good.

Every Thursday I found myself anticipating her. Her energy. Her stories. Her presence.

But Truth?

Truth was work.

Truth was a mirror I didn't want to face.

She crossed her legs, tilted her head, and exhaled dramatically.

"Let's just say my weekend was … interesting."

I noticed the mark on her neck, faint, reddish, just enough to whisper a story. I chuckled under my breath. "Truth, you know you're too grown for hickeys."

She smirked. "Oh, this? I guess I forgot to wear my scarf."

I leaned back in my chair, notebook untouched. "So, what happened?" "Uugghh, Nicol, listen," she began, eyes bright with mischief. "I met a guy after my birthday party. I was leaving the club and saw him sitting in his car, watching me. Another car pulled up, and I told them I wasn't interested. But *Him*, he just said, "I like your style, and drove off." That was it."

She paused, smiling at the memory.

"Then, early the next morning, I got a DM." *Hey, you probably don't remember me, but we met last night. I'm Him and I like the way you carry yourself.*

"We talked a bit. Turns out he's a basketball coach, well-known, respectable, the type that takes care of business. We even had mutual friends, so I felt… safe."

She glanced at me, gauging my reaction.

"I said yes to dinner and a movie. We met at the park and ride on Cottage Grove."

Her voice softened, almost dreamy. "After the movie, we just sat there and talked for an hour. He asked me the craziest thing I'd ever done, and I said… this! Then I stayed. All weekend. He made me breakfast, Nicol. He left me the keys while he coached his games. I stayed there like…"

Like what? I asked gently.

"Like I belonged."

Truth's eyes glassed over. "When the weekend ended, he drove me back to my car. We agreed to keep it simple, no strings, no questions, just bandwidth and time. Out of sight, out of mind."

She exhaled, then whispered, "But I can't get *Him* out of my head. It's like I've been rewired. I told myself I could handle casual, but… I can't. I never can. You know how I get."

Her voice trembled, just slightly. "So, do what you do and fix it."

I folded my hands. "Truth, I can't tell you what's right or wrong. My job is to give you space to think, to organize your thoughts and feelings."

She groaned, frustrated. "Why can't you just tell me what to do?"

"Do about what?", I asked, fighting the fatigue in my tone. "Having a good weekend? Enjoying the moment? Or the obsession that follows? Because you never told me what happened with the last guy."

Truth blinked. "What guy? You must have me confused."

"Oh, I don't," I snapped before I could stop myself. "This is what you do. Hook up, get attached, act confused, then repeat. So, fix what, Truth?"

The words came sharp, slicing through professionalism. My voice, or maybe not my voice, spilled out unfiltered, unrestrained. I heard myself speaking, but it didn't feel like me. Something was pushing through, raw and real.

The voice continued:
"In the past year, there've been four men. Four, Truth. What happened to them?"

Truth froze, eyes wide.

"You come in here looking for help," the voice pressed. "Then tell Nicol, tell me, what happened to the others? How did those encounters end, Truth"

Her lips quivered. The energy in the room shifted, dense and electric.

It wasn't me speaking anymore.

It was something deeper. Something that had waited for this exact moment to be heard.

It was Truth speaking through me, confronting herself.

Her eyes held storm clouds, a subtle tremor beneath her usual bravado.

She stood up and I gestured for her to sit back down on the chaise. She lowered herself, crossing her legs like a practiced queen, and immediately the tension between us thickened. I double-checked that I had my recorder on before she even spoke again.

"Okay, Nicol… I've been thinking," she began, voice steady but with an edge. "I can't stop thinking about last session."

I nodded. "Good. Thinking is the first step."

She sighed, resting her head back. "No, it's more than that. I can't… I can't stop feeling it. Like, everything we talked about, all the men, the patterns, the mistakes, it's like it's been stitched into me. And yet…" She opened her palms, as if showing invisible wounds. "…I don't remember ever deciding to stitch it there. I don't even know what's mine anymore."

I felt that familiar tightness in my chest again. The truth of her confession was cutting through the walls I'd built as a therapist, walls I had carefully maintained for years.

"Tell me what you mean," I prompted softly.

"I mean… Nicol, I feel like I'm living multiple lives at once. Like there's a part of me that's watching me, judging me, screaming at me, and yet another part just wants to disappear into the night and forget it all ever happened. And… and you…" She hesitated, eyes sharp. "Sometimes I feel like you know me better than I know myself. Like you're me, but also not me. And that scares the hell out of me."

I leaned back, letting the weight of her words settle. It wasn't the first time I'd felt this in therapy. Some of my clients were mirrors, reflecting parts of myself I didn't want to see. But Truth… she wasn't just a mirror. She was a shard. A fragment of something I had long hidden from even myself.

"Truth," I began, careful, measured. "What if… what if the parts you think are separate aren't actually separate at all?"

Her head snapped up. "What do you mean?"

I took a deep breath. "What if some of the people you've been searching for, the love, the excitement, the chaos, are actually aspects of you, asking to be recognized?"

She stared, blinking slowly, like the idea had landed in unfamiliar territory but somehow felt undeniable.

"I don't understand," she whispered.

"You've been living in fragments, Truth. Trying to reconcile experiences, pain, love, loss. You compartmentalize to survive. But all the stories, all the encounters, they are echoes of you, of me really. My voice faltered slightly. "I mean… we are connected in ways you haven't realized yet."

The room grew heavy with unspoken truths. She shifted in her seat, tugging at her hair, as if trying to pull clarity from chaos.

"You're saying I'm you?" she asked cautiously, voice cracking.

"Yes," I said quietly. "I'm saying you are a part of me. One I had buried. One I didn't want to admit even existed. But here you are, in full force, and you've been showing me the truth I didn't want to see."

Truth leaned forward, eyes blazing now. "So, all this, the men, the mistakes, the obsession, the chaos, it's mine? And I've been blaming the world for it?"

"Yes. And no. It's yours to claim, but also ours to understand. It's time to stop running from the parts of you that hurt and start integrating them. Naming them.

Seeing them. Not just hiding them in the bag, or in a story, or in a weekend fling."

The session felt like hours, though only thirty minutes had passed. Truth's defenses melted away like wax in a flame. She cried, laughed, cursed, and confessed all at once, spilling years of frustration, loneliness, and unmet needs onto the chaise.

I didn't judge. I didn't redirect. I let her unravel, fully. And through her unraveling, I began to see patterns, patterns that mirrored my own life: the grief, the survival, the longing for freedom, the reckless pursuit of love.

When the session finally ended, Truth was quieter, softer. She stood, smoothing her skirt, finally seeming more human than the whirlwind who had walked in.

"Next time," she said, almost to herself. "Next time I think we go deeper. I think I need to see the rest of me."

I nodded, knowing exactly what she meant.

The truth, our truth was about to get even more complicated.

(15)

The office smelled faintly of lavender, my recorder already humming softly on the table. Truth had left minutes ago, her energy still lingering in the air like a storm that had passed but left everything unsettled. I sat back, notebook in hand, thinking I was done for the day, when the door creaked open.

She walked in, poised, quiet, deliberate. Affinity. Even her name carried both promise and warning. I gestured to the chaise.

"Affinity," I said, voice calm. "Have a seat."

She perched herself like she owned the room, without demanding attention. Instead, she exuded it naturally, effortlessly. There was a stillness about her that drew you in, the kind of presence that made you lean forward even when you didn't want to.

"I need to start with the truth," she said softly. "I need someone to see it. I can't carry it alone anymore."

I nodded, leaning forward. "Start wherever you feel safe. I'm listening."

Her hands twisted in her lap, fingers tracing invisible patterns across the fabric of her dress. "He didn't love me. He enjoyed being loved by me."

I flinched, though I knew this line would come. This was the story I had been walking toward since the first session with Truth, the echo of my own past wrapped in someone else's voice.

"That was our pattern," she continued. "Me pouring, him receiving. Me chasing, him running. It's like therapy finally gave me the language for the push and pull we lived in. I was anxious, he was avoidant. I wanted closeness, he needed distance. The more I reached for *Him*, the more he recoiled. And yet, I kept believing that if I just held on tighter, he would see my worth and stay."

I scribbled notes, but my hands felt heavy, as if I were writing my own past. Every word she spoke mirrored old wounds I had tucked away, echoes I'd rationalized and ignored.

Affinity's eyes glimmered in the lamplight. "I can still see the blue light from my phone glowing on the nightstand as I waited for his call. The room was dark, but my chest was wide awake, tight, restless, on fire. I counted the hours he went silent, each one a fresh rejection. The silence was a monster crawling into bed with me, wrapping itself around my ribs. I'd scroll back through messages, looking for clues. Did I say too much? Did I sound needy? Did I make him feel cornered? My brain was running laps while my body lay still."

I exhaled slowly, letting the scene sink into the room. Every detail she shared, every moment of anxious expectation, was a mirror I couldn't ignore.

"When he finally did answer," she went on, voice low, almost shaking, "his voice was flat, almost bored. 'You're overthinking again,' he said. And I could practically hear the shrug. Calm, detached, like my panic was entertainment. I wanted to scream, *"Of course I'm overthinking. You disappear without explanation and expect me to act unbothered."* But instead, I swallowed my frustration and let the conversation move on. That's what I did back then. I bent to keep *Him* close."

I leaned back, silent, letting her words reverberate. Affinity's narrative wasn't just a story. It was a lesson, a warning, a reflection of every thread of unresolved attachment I had carried.

She continued, recounting dinners where his absence spoke louder than the music, meals where she affirmed and mirrored, performed and adjusted. And then, she said, voice barely a whisper, "when I tried to turn the conversation to *us,* what we were building, where we were going, his eyes dimmed. His lips pulled into a half-smile that wasn't really a smile. 'Why do you always want to talk about feelings?' he asked, leaning back like the question itself exhausted him. I laughed with him, swallowed, my chest sinking, because I had no choice."

I watched her, the story unfolding in real-time. It was mine and hers and every woman's who had been starved for reciprocity.

"One night he handed me a box," she said. "Small, glossy, expensive. I knew before opening it, a watch. Cold, foreign. I traced it with my finger. And he waited for my excitement, for my validation. I didn't want it. I just needed him. And that was the moment I saw it, his panic, the blankness, the way his shoulders stiffened like I had asked for something he didn't own. That was his kryptonite."

Affinity's eyes were dark pools now, shadows of old grief reflected back at me. "The relationship started unraveling," she whispered, "not with explosions, but with threads slowly coming undone. I stopped letting him buy my silence. I stopped clapping for the bare minimum. And the more I pulled back, the clearer it became, there was no real partnership underneath."

I exhaled, finally. "And what hurts most?" I asked gently.

"What hurts most," she said, eyes glistening, "was realizing how little I valued myself in the process. How I made his inability to love me a reflection of my worth, when it was just a reflection of his limitations. I thought persistence was loyalty, forgiveness was strength. But it was just teaching me to tolerate breadcrumbs."

I nodded slowly, recorder clicking softly. "And now?" I asked.

Affinity leaned back, a faint smile curving her lips. "I'm healing. I'm learning that real love doesn't hide. Real love doesn't punish you for being soft or present. Real love doesn't need distance to feel safe. I still have pieces of *Him* in my heart but love alone isn't enough anymore. I need reciprocity. Safety. Ease. And when it comes, I'll recognize it because it will feel like peace, not panic."

That session ended with quiet understanding. But as I tidied my notes, a creeping realization began to settle in. The pattern was too familiar, the anxious pursuit, the mirrored avoidance, the relentless hope for love that didn't exist in the form I needed. It wasn't just Affinity's story.

It was mine.

And just like with Truth, just like with Nostalgia, I had begun the slow, careful work of seeing myself in my clients, in their pain, their patterns, their longings.

I knew the next session would change everything. It was time to meet Affinity fully, not just as a client, but as a reflection of the parts of me I had been too afraid to acknowledge.

The office felt quieter than usual. The faint hum of the heater and the soft scratch of my pen against paper were the only sounds. I sat on the chaise, recorder running, my notebook open but empty. I wasn't sure what to expect.

Affinity walked in first, calm and poised as always. Her presence carried that same steady weight, but I noticed the subtle tension in her shoulders.

Truth walked in restless and raw. She wasn't loud, but she was heavy. I could feel the weight she carried from across the room.

Later, Nostalgia appeared without warning, lingering like a shadow at the edge of the room. I sensed they would all come together today.

Silence.

I looked toward the door expectantly. But she never walked in.

Swez.

Affinity sat down, folding her hands neatly in her lap. "Nicol," she said softly, "I feel… I feel fractured. I don't know who I am without them, without Nostalgia, without Truth. I thought I knew, but…" Her voice trailed off.

I nodded slowly, letting the space breathe. "Take a deep breath. We'll work through it together."

And then, as if drawn by some invisible cue, the others echoed fragments of emotion and memory, each one demanding recognition.

Nostalgia's lingering grief, Truth's restless chaos, Affinity's longing for balance.

And I realized, with a jolt that was both terrifying and liberating, they weren't separate from me.

They were me.

Nostalgia's voice whispered in the back of my mind, sharp and emotional: "You can't help me. You can't fix this."

Truth's frustration rose behind it, impatient and relentless:
"Why won't you just tell me what to do?"

And Affinity, steady and reflective, reminded me:
"You have to see all of us. You have to see yourself."

I closed my eyes, letting the voices swell and mix. I could feel each of them, every fragment of my past and present trauma, every pattern of love, loss, betrayal, and hope. The reality hit me like a wave: I had been my own client all along.

I spoke aloud, shakily at first, then with growing clarity. "I see you. I see all of you. I see me."

The room shifted. The weight of decades of fear, grief, longing, and self-denial lifted slightly. I let the tears fall, for the widow, the lonely lover, the anxious daughter, the woman who had chased, forgiven, hoped, and survived. I named each one as they stood up and walked out of the room.

Nostalgia. Truth. Affinity. Swez.

She had been there all along.

And I realized, finally, the truth of Post-Traumatic Relationship Disorder wasn't just about romantic entanglements.

It was about me navigating life in fragments, interacting with the world through pieces of myself that I didn't fully integrate.

I reached for the recorder, pressing stop. I didn't need to record this moment. It was mine.

And as I exhaled, a profound clarity settled over me.

Nostalgia represented grief, loss, and longing for the love I'd buried.

Truth represented chaos, desire, and the unbridled recklessness of emotional survival.

Affinity represented recognition, the desire for authentic connection, and the slow, painful realization of my own worth.

Swez represented freedom, indulgence, the courage to live boldly, to break the rules for myself.

I smiled, knowing I didn't need to chase any more. I didn't need to beg for validation. I didn't need to reconstruct a lost past.

I was whole because I was willing to face all parts of myself.

I opened my notebook, writing with deliberate care:

"I am all of these things. I am grief and joy, chaos and calm, desire, and discernment. I am fractured and whole. I am me. I will not ignore my intuition. I will not stay where I am not respected or appreciated. I will not let loneliness talk me into love.

For the first time in years, I felt peace. The fractured selves weren't enemies. They were teachers, guides, and mirrors. Each had a story, each had lessons and together, they had brought me back to myself.

The office felt lighter. The soft hum of the heater no longer seemed like background noise, it felt like a heartbeat. And I realized I was ready to live, fully and unapologetically. In the space where every part of me belonged.

Weeks later, I returned to my Thursday ritual. My quiet dinners, my favorite bar, the music that had once carried me to Swez, to joy, to liberation. But this time I went alone, truly alone and truly present.

I walked in and I didn't need anyone to show up. I didn't need notes on my windshield. I didn't need external validation. The woman in the mirror reflected a single truth: I was complete.

Life would continue to bring challenges. Love would come and go, people would leave. The world would shift. But I faced myself. I had untangled the knots of my past, embraced the chaos and the joy, and discovered that I had everything I needed already.

PTRD taught me the most important lesson of all: the most enduring relationship in life isn't romantic, transactional, or fleeting. It is the relationship you have with yourself.

And with that, I smiled, poured myself a fresh drink and danced alone, whole, and finally free.

Act IX

The Final Pause

The quiet that teaches the art of release.

A "friend," someone I'd known for decades, accused me of theft, a betrayal that cut deeper than the lie itself.

Truth is, what they had accused me of was worth as much as wooden nickels, pennies compared to the cash I had access to.

The betrayal that came with that accusation deepened the fracture.
To be accused of something so petty, it would've been laughable if it hadn't cut so deep. It wasn't about the money. It was about loyalty. About realizing that people you *love* don't always love you with the same integrity.

That realization shattered the foundation I thought was unbreakable. It cracked something open. They didn't cause the cracks though. Nah. I'd never give them that much credit.

I didn't even mourn or grieve the "loss" of that "friendship".
Actually, they made me realize that they meant about as much to me as I meant to them.
In that moment, their betrayal was a turning point, a catalyst that forced me to examine every single "ship" in my life: friendship, sisterhood, family, work… intimacy.

Every connection came under a microscope.

I examined every situation where I had poured too much and never asked for recognition. Some "ships" were toxic. Some were unsteady. Some, I realized, I'd been holding together with nothing but my own strength.

So, I shut down, completely.
Social media. Social life. Business. Writing. Everything stopped.
I did the bare minimum to exist, enough to function, enough to "have it."

I went through the motions because I had to, because my now adult children still depended on me, but I stopped pretending for the world.

For the first time, I allowed myself to collapse in the safety of my own space.

I remember it clearly. For months after work, I went upstairs at four o'clock, and that was it. My bed became my sanctuary, my confessional, my escape. I slept there, cried there, ate there, and sometimes wished to dissolve into nothingness. Figuratively, not literally, I wanted to dry up and scatter like ashes.

I gained another thirty pounds on top of the extra fifty I'd already carried, a physical manifestation of the burdens I had been holding silently for over a decade.

Some major life choices I made, and the pandemic didn't help.

But no one noticed. Or at least, I thought no one did.

And then came the texts.
"Sis, checking in on you."
"Col."
"Col, I'm just checking in on you."
"Nicol".
"Nicol, I haven't seen you on social just checking in to make sure you are ok. I miss seeing your posts of encouragement."

Small words. Tiny lifelines. Reminders that I wasn't invisible.

Even in my darkest pause, people who genuinely cared reminded me that I mattered.

They didn't demand explanations. They didn't ask me to perform strength. They simply showed up.

That consistency, that quiet attention, was a lifeboat in the storm.

Some "ships" never returned from the pause. There was no repair. Sometimes an ending isn't dramatic; sometimes it's quiet, gradual, leaving a hollow that no apology can fill.

But that hollow made room for the real friends, the ones who showed up without fail, the ones who said "I got you" and meant it.

And slowly, I did it. I started moving again, intentionally this time.

The weight dropped. My energy returned. My smile came easier. I laughed. I cried without shame.

I started choosing relationships that nurtured, rather than drained.

I reclaimed my joy.
I rediscovered the parts of myself I had forgotten in the shadows of responsibility: curiosity, boldness, pleasure, play, travel.

By the end of that pause, I was no longer just *having it*. I was *living it*.

I was Col.

Whole. Vibrant. Unafraid. Unapologetically Human.

I was learning to release the hyper-independence (to a point), to trust others, to trust myself, to receive love and support without guilt, to respect my boundaries.

I learned that real strength isn't endurance alone. It's balance, self-awareness, and the courage to lean when you need to. It's self-love, and knowing your worth isn't validated by any outside source.

The Final Pause became a pivotal chapter in my life.
It taught me that it's okay to be weak.
That vulnerability is not a liability, it's the bridge to authenticity.
That self-love isn't selfish, it's necessary.
That strength isn't measured in silence or stoicism, but in the grace to allow yourself to be fully seen.

And as I look back now, I see the threads of connection that carried me:
My children who held space for me without judgment.
My Mom for her prayers and strength.
The seasons of romance that cradled me between the illusion of safety and the ache of unpredictability—the love I gave my heart to, believing it was forever, but wasn't.
The friendships that ended, leaving room for the right people to step in.

Each of them, each moment, each pause, was part of the architecture of my healing.

I paused, and in that pause, I found Swez, Nostalgia, Truth, Affinity and the Therapist.

I found myself.

And for the first time, I didn't just *have them.*
They had me.

Epilogue

Because endings are only beginnings in disguise.

After the final session with the alters, I found myself sitting quietly in the therapist chair, alone.

The room was dim, the recorder off, yet I could still feel the echoes of every story I had held, every fragment of myself I had uncovered. Each alter, each memory, each unspoken truth had left its mark.

I faced myself in every mirror, in every voice.

I exhaled slowly and realized something I hadn't fully acknowledged,
I had finally arrived.

Not at an ending, not at a conclusion, but at a threshold.

I had been the woman who survived, who confronted her fears, who faced loss and heartbreak and still found the courage to keep showing up.

But now, standing in that quiet space after therapy, I understood that my story had only been the first act.

And then she arrived.

Two years had passed since those last therapy sessions ended.

Life had changed in ways both subtle and seismic.

She was the embodiment of everything I had been striving toward but hadn't yet fully claimed.

She moved with calm confidence, a softness and lightness that spoke of self-love and self-worth.

She didn't just exist, she thrived.

She had no need for external validation, yet she welcomed connection and joy freely.

She smiled at the world, and in her smile, I saw the full reflection of my journey.

She had the courage to step into life on her own terms, to embrace possibility without hesitation, and to love without fear.

Every lesson from therapy. Every encounter with Swez, Nostalgia, Truth, and Affinity had led to this moment.

She was not just me, she was my evolution.

I watched her take the first steps of this new chapter, knowing that this story, my story, *our story,* was far from over.

The journey continued, but now with a guide who understood the value of peace, reciprocity, and self-respect.

She was my promise to myself,
That life could be fully claimed, fully lived, and fully loved on my own terms.

And as she moved forward, I felt a quiet thrill of anticipation.

As she approached, I asked her name.
She smiled and said "Hi, I'm NOE."

And that's when I knew…
This was not the end.

It was the beginning of our ***Second Act***.

Till next time,

Ni' out…

Author Spotlight

Nicol NOE McClendon

Nicol NOE McClendon is a dynamic public speaker, creative visionary, and literary voice whose work centers on healing, identity, and transformation.

Her debut novella, *The Therapist Chair*, marks a powerful entry into the world of narrative healing—blending personal truth with fictional depth to explore Post-Traumatic Relationship Disorder and the journey back to self.

With a background rooted in resilience and grace, Nicol's storytelling invites readers to confront emotional truths and reclaim their self-worth. Her writing is both a mirror and a movement, offering women a space to be seen, heard, and empowered.

Nicol's message is clear: *"The end is a new beginning"* is not just a subtitle—it's a call to action.

Her work champions:

- Healing after emotional and spiritual trauma
- Choosing peace over chaos
- Guarding your pour
- Redefining strength through softness
- Finding yourself again in your own reflection

The Therapist Chair is more than a story—it's a movement. A call to heal, to choose peace, and to redefine strength through softness.

Nicol believes the end is never final—it's the beginning of becoming.

Connect With the Author

Thank you for reading. Your support means everything. If this book inspired you, moved you, or opened something within you, stay connected with Nicol and continue the journey.

Website
www.nicolmcclendon.com

Facebook
Author Nicol McClendon

Instagram
Author Nicol McClendon

Email
AuthorNicolMcClendon@gmail.com

Your story matters. Your voice deserves to be heard. Stay connected and keep writing.

Also by Nicol McClendon

NONFICTION

It's My Story I Will Tell It: Pieces of Me

It's Your Story Tell It: The Writers Journal

**Blessed Not Broken (Vol1): Journey to
Finding Purpose in Marriage, Motherhood &
Entrepreneurship as a CEO Wife (co-author)**

**Matters of the Heart: My Journey
Surviving 10 years and 5 months on the
Heart Transplant List (co-author)**